Merry Christmas!

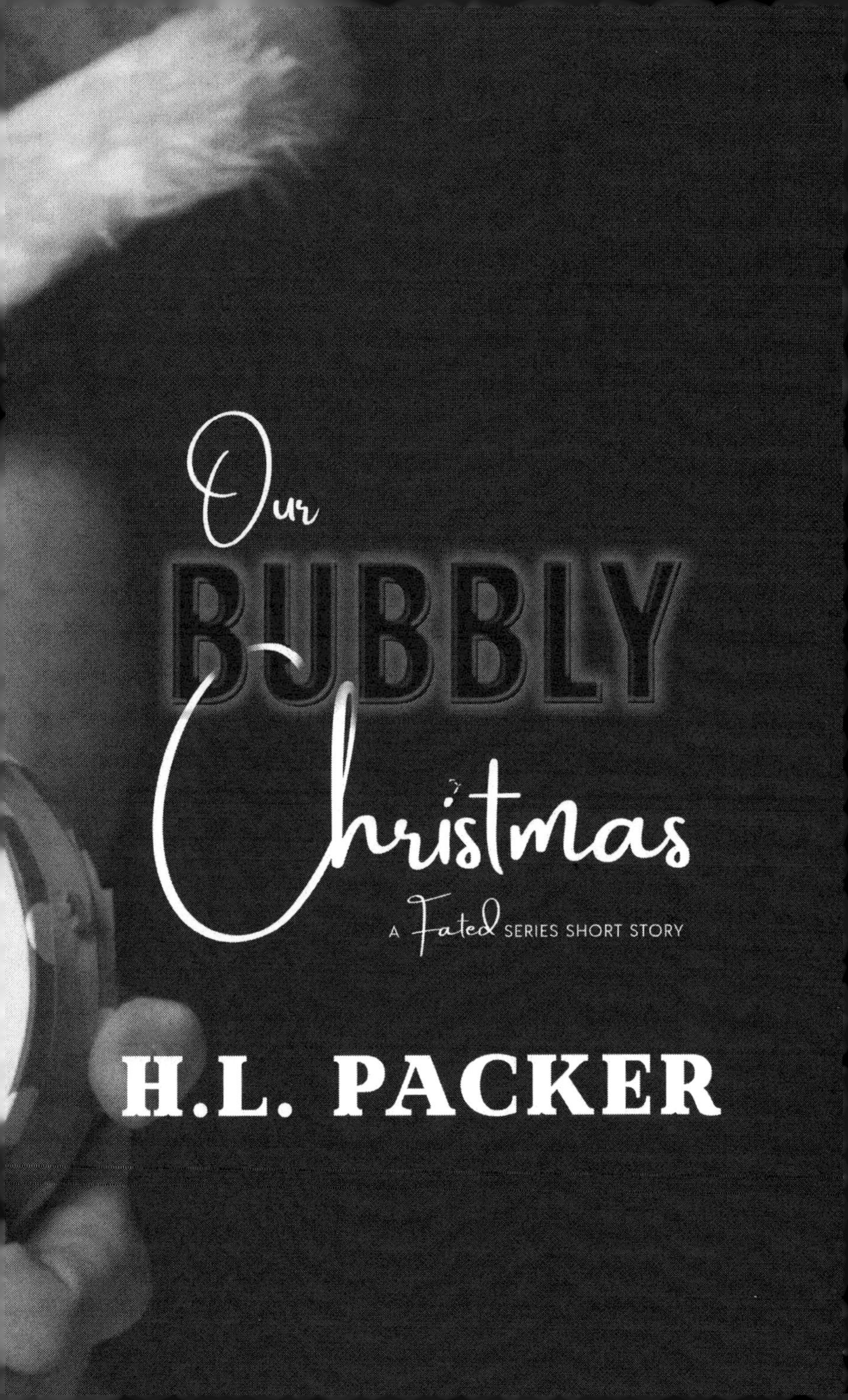
Our
BUBBLY
Christmas
A Fated SERIES SHORT STORY
H.L. PACKER

Editor – Vicki James of The Indie Hub

Cover Designer – LJDesigns

Formatter – LJDesigns

ONE
Vittoria

Holy Fuck.

Aftershocks ripple over my body while he holds my thighs apart, his wicked tongue flicking and sucking at my oversensitive flesh even as he continues to thrust lazily in my mouth from beneath me.

"God, you taste good," he praises, the vibration of his deep voice rippling through me as an uncontrollable shudder wracks over my body. *He always gets me hot and heavy in sixty-nine.*

My nails dig into his leg and ass, taking him as deeply as I can, sucking and bobbling until he eventually lets me go and drops his head back against the sheets, something akin to a moan escaping him.

"Hold up," he says between panted breaths, tapping my ass.

I release him, and he shuffles over, reaching into the drawer and rifling around for a condom. Moving on shaky legs I sit, watching with fascination as he sheaths himself, the latex covering him from base to tip and sliding as he tugs up and down slowly.

Unfortunately, there's no time to savour the anticipation as my morning alarm blares yet again. Blindly, I knock it off, way more interested in what he's doing while I wait for him to be ready before seating myself over his cock, his lips pressing against mine with urgency.

Our moans of pleasure entwine, the feeling of fullness divine as I lift and grind against him, one orgasm barely receding before the next one is building, twisting and turning in my core with this new angle. His hands fall to my hips as he thrusts up hard, chasing oblivion.

"That's it, baby. So fucking amazing."

He fucks, I rub, and the two of us come so hard I see stars, just in time for his phone to ring.

"Jesus, this better be fucking important," he complains, still shuddering beneath me even as he reaches for it, stilling when he see's who it is. "Fuck. Sorry, baby."

I climb off him, knowing exactly what that look means. His clipped answers and cold tone tell me exactly who's on the other end of the line: *La Famiglia*.

A chill creeps over me, the sweat cooling on my still damp skin. Climbing from the tangle of cream sheets is an effort, as is falling into the bathroom and turning on the shower, but I manage it, giving him the space to take his call.

The warm water lulls me back into reality and has me remembering that I'm now running late. Hurrying my steps, I wash up quickly, finding Franky holding a fluffy tower out for me when I climb out. He wraps me up warmly before placing a quick kiss on my lips and jumping in himself. No words are required, only that smirk that's never far from his lips.

And just like we did yesterday—as well as a few days before that, and a few days before that, too—we fall into what's quickly becoming *our* morning routine. I brush my teeth and get dressed, knowing he's already put the coffee on, before grabbing a couple of biscotti and the last of the soft fruit.

"I'll have to run by the shops after work," I say idly, looking over the bare bones remaining in the fridge. "There's no way this lot is going to be enough to make it through Christmas week."

"Don't forget I did that online order for you. It'll be here between six and seven," Franky says, his dark eyes twinkling as he grabs his mug, then winks. *His mug.*

Those black trousers fit him way too well, his ass too perfect for words when encased in the made-for-him suit. He fastens the worn, brown leather belt one-handed whilst simultaneously finding a coaster for his mug, like he's done it a million times before.

"I thought you were spending Christmas with your family?" I ask.

"Yeah, well, Sofia called to say that one of the kids has some kind of plague, and Lola is going to her boyfriend's house." He practically coughs out the word *boyfriend*, almost refusing to acknowledge it. "I'll be joining mia famiglia on Boxing Day, as always, but if your plans haven't changed, perhaps we could spend it together?"

He fastens the crisp, white shirt without looking at me, belying the vulnerability in his question as he waits for an answer. His Adam's apple bobs as he swallows nervously before turning away.

Twenty million things flicker through my brain, not a single one of them managing to tumble from my lips.

"Franky, I—"

Why aren't the words coming?

Yes, my parents are still away.

"Or not," he says, cutting me off before he thinks I'll reject him, no doubt. "Don't worry about it. Alessia always has space at her table. What's an extra day, right?"

No, I couldn't imagine anything better than spending Christmas Day with you.

He shrugs the waistcoat over his shoulders like it's a second skin, then the holster, too, as he checks the guns before strapping them in safely and reaching for his jacket, his disappointment crackling in the air.

"I wish the kids were more excited about Christmas." I blurt the words out—the thought as much of a surprise to me as they are to him, if the confused look he pins me with is anything to go by as his jacket hangs limply over his arm.

Rounding the kitchen island brings me within reaching distance of him, and I force my feet to slow, not rushing to him like my heart wants to, even now.

He watches the sway of my hips and the swish in my skirt, his gaze setting fire to my blood as it sizzles over my tits, eventually rising to meet my own. I'll make this right with him, but I have to explain this random thought before we get there as I scramble to make sense of it myself.

"They're only interested in whatever ridiculously overpriced games thing they think they can get their hands on. Whatever happened to baby Jesus? To Midnight Mass?" I ask, adjusting his tie for him, even though it's already perfect. I just need to touch him—to be near. "When did they forget about Santa?"

"Santa?" he repeats.

I nod. "It's the last day of school; Christmas Jumper Day." I gesture to the genteel, snowflake scarf folded on the counter. "And not a single one of them will come in something silly." Not that I am, either, but still.

I don't know when the fun of Christmas disappeared for them, but it's been way too long since I saw my class laugh at something genuinely funny and not someone pulling themselves or other people apart for likes.

I know it's not the declaration Franky was looking for, and I can feel his disappointment, even if his features don't show it. No, he's way too controlled to let himself slip.

Perhaps the regret is my own, not his.

"Was I an entitled little shit, too?" he asks, mischief twirling in those dark irises as he pushes past whatever he's really feeling.

"Absolutely." I nod again. "The worst."

Don't get me wrong, I've watched this group of kids grow and change over the last however many months it has been, none of them children in the first place. They're teens—young adults who are practically men and women—but it helps me to compartmentalise it if they're children, young people, or students.

I made the mistake of treating the children like adults in one of my first years of teaching. It's hard because technically they are, but that's what got me in this situation in the first place. There was this one boy. He was a man long before he should have been, and he called me out and pushed my buttons. He was relentless.

Oh, I have no doubt that he was telling his friends how

I fell at his feet and made him '*work for that A+*', but the truth is, he has a brilliant mind and never once needed my help. He could have gone on to do amazing things under different circumstances, but couldn't we both?

Not that working at the most prestigious school around is an issue. No, the money is good, the job is easy, and mostly, the students don't give me any shit. That wouldn't be the case at the school I should have gone to a few years ago; the one with the awful reputation where my work would have been harder but more impactful.

It's also over a hundred miles away.

Whilst I'm aware La Famiglia has a large reach, I'm not sure it's that far, and wasn't that the draw in the first place?

Originally, I applied when we were on one of our *off* moments, and there've been a few of them, historically speaking. It would have been a chance to get away from him, to start afresh, but then life happened and we fell back together, so the job came and went.

I know he's not walking away from them; La Famiglia. He can't. So, he's here, I'm here, and even as I watch the thoughts flicker behind his eyes, I know he wants to stay, to choose us over everything, but he can't. He has a job to do, and so do I.

"I must have been really charming," Franky replies with a smirk, reminding me so much of the teenage version of him, only a few years younger than me but still young enough. It's a look that's developed and changed, much like the man himself—the one that was doing things much more nefarious than fucking his teacher at eighteen.

"You still are," I reply.

"I totally get it," he says, holding his tie out for me to look at.

"Are those snowmen?" I ask with a smile.

"Yep."

A chuckle falls free as I hold the silky material in my fingers. His hands are hot at my waist.

"I'd love it if you could join me for Christmas," I admit, catching his intense gaze and the feelings that neither of us are willing to admit out loud.

He nods, a smile creeping across his handsome face before he brings his lips to mine. His tongue tangles, tasting and deepening the kiss briefly before he pulls back and steps away.

"Sounds like a plan. Don't forget there'll be food here between six and seven."

Part of me loves that he doesn't make a big deal of it. It's just a few days together, something we do all the time, and I've often wondered why he even keeps his place when we spend so much time here. But I'm also aware it's Christmas, and that feels like it's kind of a big deal.

"I'll be here," I agree. His hand stills on the door handle. "We're not doing gifts, though, right? Because last year we said that, and then we both did… but I honestly haven't gotten you anything at all this time, so I just want to be sure."

"Absolutely." He nods, coming back to finish his coffee. "I'll be back late, though. Probably nineish, if that's okay?"

"Yeah, that's fine. I'll sort out the food and then get ready for drinks." I move back to the safety of the kitchen and grab my coffee.

"Cool, see you tonight. Oh, you might want to get a move on. We're late." And with that as his leaving remark, he winks and closes the door just as a notification flashes on my phone, illuminating the time.

"Shit."

TWO
Franky

Late is not a word written in the Mariotti handbook, if such a thing were to even exist, and as the engine rumbles to life beneath me and the clock flashes up on the dashboard, I realise I'm going to need to haul ass to make it in time, or pray to God for some kind of non-fatal delay.

Obviously, I'd never wish harm on my nearest and dearest, but if there happened to be some signal tower miscommunication that left them circling in the air for say… twenty minutes, that wouldn't be the end of the world, right?

Luckily for me, Vittoria's place is closer to the airfield than mine, giving me a head start. I fly down the familiar roads, making good time before pulling into the strip with just minutes to spare, my brain ticking through our conversation.

So, nobody is making a thing about Christmas at the school any more.

Not that we did what we were supposed to for ninety percent of our time there, but we sure as hell threw on a stupid jumper when it was Christmas… or a tie, or a waistcoat or something. The dress code was bullshit anyway, so any excuse to throw something random in there was always a win with me.

"You're cutting it close," one of the guys comments as I climb from the car, tipping the sunglasses to the top of his head before pushing off the car and coming over to greet me.

"Nah, timed it perfectly," I reply, just as the plane taxi's to a stop. "Is it just the two of us?"

"Arturo is just pulling around. He had to get some kind of iced coffee or something."

"Iced?"

"Yeah, I don't get it, either, but you know what Carlos is like. When he wants something, you just do it."

The other car pulls up, and Arturo climbs out with a tray of drinks in his hand, nodding my way as the three of us wait for the doors to open and the guests to disembark.

But suddenly, I have an idea.

Knowing I only have a few minutes before they're out and expecting me, I climb back into the car, grab my phone and pull up a search engine to find a fancy dress shop nearby. Without giving myself chance to second guess it, I press call, and a harried sounding woman eventually answers.

"Hey, I realise it's a little last-minute, but do you have any Santa costumes available?" I ask.

I know we said no presents, but this wouldn't count, would it?

"On Christmas Eve?"

"Ah, yeah," I reply, watching the doors open and the hostess step out onto the ladder. Time is running out, quickly.

"Yeah, we've racks and racks available. Come pick out what you like," she says sarcastically.

"Really?"

"No. Try again next year in good time." The line goes dead.

Well, that was fucking rude.

Disappointment sinks to the bottom of my stomach as I climb out of the car, waiting with everyone else while we watch Carlos help Sophie down the stairs.

It's got bigger over the last few years, this group of ours. Once upon a time, it was just me and Tino, Anton and Carlos—just four friends fucking around—but when one of your best friends is the heir to the mafia throne, life gets busy fast.

Tino and I spent as much time in the Mariotti home as we did in our own growing up. More so as teenagers. And these days… well, whilst plenty of things have changed, breakfast at the house is still a staple, even if it doesn't end up being daily, or breakfast.

When Carlos went to London to persue Sophie (on famiglia business, of course) Tino went with him. And when Tino fell in love with Niamh—a casualty of the war we raged over there—he stayed there with them, too, for a while. Anton and I had responsibilities here, so we stayed.

But Niamh's brother was already here and attempting to hide his relationship with Carlos's sister. Yeah, shit gets complicated quickly, and Sophie's brother needed an eye keeping on him over there, so we ended up in different places. The division was never intentional, I don't think, just kind of how it fell.

"Tell me one of you guys has a baby seat with them…" I ask, watching Andrew's girlfriend adjust the blanket around a tiny bundle that must be their newborn.

"Yes," they both reply.

"At least we've got that covered."

Sophie's mother follows, with Andrew looking like he's ready to throw her from the plane… or maybe that's just how he always looks. Then there's Tino and Niamh trailing behind.

It's been way too long since we had everyone together, and, cancelled family plans or not, I know there'll be a celebration worth taking part in with these guys. I guess it's going to have to wait until Boxing Day, though.

Excitement tickles my extremities as I think of her there with us.

I know Vittoria has never been a fan of La Famiglia and the businesses we're in. It's part of who I am, who I always have been, so she's accepted that, but she's never wanted to be involved with that side of my life. Having her sat at the table with me on Boxing Day is something I could never imagine until this moment.

My best friends and their wives and girlfriends, and me, with the woman who's stood beside me for the past, well, too many years, I suppose. It was never meant to be a thing between us. She was a teacher and I was a student and while fucking one of my teachers was a dream come true, I never expected that it would continue.

And yet, continue it has. Even when she got pissed off about the late nights and the early mornings, the jobs and assignments I couldn't tell her about, the trips across the country, and further afield. So we broke up, and we got back together, and we repeated that more than once because there's something about that woman that I can't let go.

Sure, I might do things she doesn't approve of, but I'm a good man underneath all that, and I think she knows it. I hope she does.

She's the most beautiful woman I've ever set my eyes on, and that's saying something for the amazing women that throw themselves at famiglia men. She's kind, and considerate, she always puts others before herself, and I know, beyond the shadow of a doubt, that she's the only person I'd ever consider bringing to the famiglia table.

No matter what she thinks she knows about the work we do, when she finally see's the family we are, she'll understand. She'll see what I see when I look at these men and their partners. This isn't a just group of stone-cold killers standing around and talking about the weather, this is family.

"What's got you smiling from ear to ear at this time of day?" Tino asks, ambling over and pulling me in to slap his hand on my back.

"Just some girl," I reply nonchalantly. He wouldn't get it. She used to be 'just some girl', but she isn't anymore and hasn't been for a long time.

"And that's probably all we need to know about that," he says, cutting off the conversation there and pulling Niamh in under his arm. I've cultured the playboy reputation all these years, finally it's coming in useful.

I greet Niamh with a smile and a nod, knowing all about her problems with people getting too close to her. Sophie brushes past, heading straight for Arturo before handing out the iced coffee. Interestingly, Niamh doesn't seem to shirk back from her prescence like she would have done once upon a time. *The girl is making progress.*

"Now, I don't mean to be rude, but which one of you young men will be taking us back to the house? It's freezing out here," Sophie's mother Francesca interrupts.

"Uh, I need to check in with Anton at Gusto first," Carlos says. "Sophie, would you be okay setting everyone up back at the house?"

"Of course." She smiles, kissing him quickly before swooping in for the baby. "It would be my pleasure."

Arturo manages to get the baby—Hope, I think she's called—Andrew, his girlfriend who's name I really should remember, Sophie, and Francesca strapped in and on their way whilst Carlos taps away on his phone.

"Are you guys going home?" I ask Tino.

He looks at Niamh before nodding, an entire conversation passing between them without words being spoken aloud. "I guess that means you're on Carlos duty," he says, knowing Carlos will want me over some random driver and ushering her into the other car. "We'll catch up soon though, yeah?"

"Sure thing," I agree, watching them climb in. Carlos taps away furiously on his phone while I unlock the car, moving that way. "So, Gusto. Is everything okay?"

"Yeah, fine. It's just been a long flight with that woman complaining about every damn thing," he grumbles, jumping in the front with me.

There are no airs and graces between us. Not usually, anyway. Anton might ride in the back with Tino now, but I guess that's different with him being the official head of the family. We've been friends for so many years, sometimes it's hard to remember they're a target and not just two guys riding around. But the guns strapped to me are there for a reason—one we've had cause to use in the past.

"Can you call Pops?" Carlos asks, still clicking away on his phone.

Not that anyone in their right mind would call Luca Mariotti '*Pops*' if they wanted to keep their tongue in their head.

"Sure thing," I reply, pressing to return the last call as I start up the engine.

"Isla's Costumes, how can I help you?" echoes around the cabin. *Shit.*

"Sorry, wrong number," I rush out, quickly ending the call.

"You getting dressed up for us, Franky?" Carlos asks with a smile, his phone forgotten for the moment.

"Abso-fucking-lutely not." I pull up Luca's number and call. "It was a last-minute surprise for a friend, but they're all out, so never mind."

"If you're calling me with a problem, try Anton," Luca complains when he answers. "That's what I pay you lot for."

"Nice to speak to you, too, father," Carlos says dryly. "I'm heading straight to Gusto, but I thought doing an impromptu induction with Andrew whilst he's here might be a good idea."

"It is," he replies, the thoughts clearly swirling around in his head, even from this distance. "Talk to your cousin about it, he's in charge, but it sounds like a plan to me."

"Oh, whilst you're here, have you still got that old Santa costume somewhere?" Carlos asks his father.

"Shut up," I hiss under my breath, my eyes widening in mortification.

"Probably," Luca replies, not even giving a fuck that this has nothing to do with anything. "You'd have to speak with your mother about it. She sorts all that stuff out."

"Cool. Thanks, Pop."

The call goes dead, and I can not believe Carlos just asked that.

"Do you really think that's going to fit me? Even if Alessia had time to go and find it, which I'm sure she won't with everyone arriving any minute, Luca and I are not exactly the same size or shape."

No disrespect intended, he's been the head of Famiglia Mariotti for a long time. He's been our surrogate father, mentor, support, boss. The man has been more things to more people than you could name, but he's way rounder in the stomach department than I am.

"You don't have to use it." Carlos shrugs. "But what's your other option?"

Good point.

"Will you speak to Alessia for me, please?" I grumble, knowing he's right.

"No, but I'll ask Tia," he replies with a smirk, his fingers flying across his phone screen as he no doubt texts her.

She's not exactly known for being discreet.

This is going to be the talk of Christmas.

Fucking great.

***

"So, what exactly do you need this for?" Tia asks, shaking the jacket out.

"It's for a friend," I say evasively. Not that I think avoiding the question will work with her, but it's worth a try. Tia has some kind of magic way of getting information out of you, and she always has. "It's a favour for a friend."

"Are you volunteering to go around the local hospitals or something? Did someone drop out?" She sprays some kind of spritz over it while I'm perched on the edge of the sofa, really just wanting to get out of here so I can go pick up the other thing I need before the shop closes.

"Not quite."

"Come on, you've got to spill the details now I've spent all that time rummagaing around in the dust on Christmas Eve. I'm supposed to be in a party dress drinking cocktails."

"Tia, it's eleven in the morning." I sigh.

"Still stands." She shrugs. "I want cocktails and pretty shoes."

This fucking woman. Always with the shoes.

"Details, please." She swishes her hair over her shoulder, pinning me with a pleading look that I'm sure works every damn time, and not just on her father and her boyfriend Cian.

"Fine," I grumble. "It's a surprise for a girl."

"I knew it." She grins like the cat that got the cream. "Well, I'd have liked to have had it washed first, but we don't have time for it to dry." She fluffs something up and straightens the bobble on the end of the hat before handing it over. "Don't get anything gross on it, please."

"I don't know what you all take me for," I say, mock offended.

"How about the man-whore we all know and love?" She

smiles, kissing me quickly on the cheek before escaping to the twenty million jobs that I know she has on today.

It's Christmas Eve in a house that will be serving what no doubt feels like a million people tomorrow. I'm surprised she was even able to make time for this. And I'm grateful.

"Thank you!" I call to her retreating form, but she waves me off like it's no big deal.

Now, time to get the last part of this surprise picked up, oh, and the work done.

THREE
Vittoria

"So, he told you no gifts, and you believed him?" Maria asks from the sofa, the pristine leather creaking when she moves.

"Oh, we've all fallen for that one," Carla says. "You don't get him anything because you take him at his word, then *he* looks like the big man when he brings you some generic gift that took no thought or effort. But you're too busy beating yourself up about not getting him anything to think about it. Classic."

"Well, we did say we wouldn't get anything last year and then we both did, but I'm sure it'll be fine." I wave them off, insecurity swimming in my stomach. *What if he does turn up with something?*

Not that I think Franky would ever give me something thoughtless or generic, but there was something about the way he left this morning that definitely suggested he had something in mind. Fuck.

"I knew I should have got him that watch," I grumble, crossing one leg over the other.

It was perfect. Not only because it was in a little store just outside of town so he wouldn't have seen it, but it was just so *him* that I couldn't even explain it, but because we weren't doing gifts, I didn't get it. What an idiot!

"You'll probably struggle to get anything now," Maria

says. "Most of the shops will be closing in half an hour."

"Thanks for the good news."

"But all your classes are done for the day, so you could go and grab something if you're quick," Carla says encouragingly. "It might have to be a generic supermarket purchase, but that's better than nothing, right?"

"We're supposed to be here for the staff Christmas event, though," I tell her, looking at the clock.

"It's not compulsory," Maria says, brushing me off. "And we'll cover for you… unless you'd rather stay here and not get your man a gift."

"He's not my man…" officially. "It's complicated." Not least because he used to be my student here at The Academy.

"I know it's one of the better staff events of the year, and I promise I'll grab your favour bag and drop it off for you," Maria says. "But, go… don't be the loser with no gift. That is not the way to start your Christmas break."

Indecision swirls through me as I watch the clock again, the minutes ticking down.

I could go and get him something—anything—or I could stay here and do the things I'm supposed to be doing in the place I'm supposed to be… but don't *have* to be.

"Are you sure?" I ask.

"Absolutely. Go!"

I ponder it for another full minute before standing, thanking them, then leaving.

What are friends for if not helping you out in a last-minute bind?

A quick Google search shows the shop where I'd seen the pocket watch is closed already. As are the other two places I had in the back of my mind. *I really thought there would be somewhere open still.*

I guess that means I'm going generic after all.

Unfortunately, but unsurprisingly, the car park is heaving when I get there, with more people coming out than going in messing up the whole thing. It takes forever to get parked as I watch the minutes tick by to closing time, but I manage to get in just at the last second, the security guard huffing grumpily.

As I look around, though, dread sinks into the pit of my stomach. Every bunch of flowers is gone or half-dead, the discounted bundles the best of a bad lot, but I'm not sure they're exactly his thing.

Think.

Think.

Think.

What does he like?

Fizzy pop, and that lager.

I'm sure it tastes mostly like soap, but I bet they have some of those left…

The fresh fruit and vegetables are completely ravaged as I rush from one aisle to the next, bypassing the confectionary. Luckily, they have one last bundle of lager bottles on the shelf, and I manage to snag them alongside a twin-pack of Coke.

It's not perfect by any stretch of the imagination, but I guess it'll do.

Making it out of the car park is as arduous as getting in was, and I make it home just in time for the delivery Franky ordered. There's everything you could possibly need for a romantic weekend at home stashed in the order: wine, chocolate, cheese, all the Christmas staples. He even remembered the Prosecco I like.

For a man who wasn't going to be spending the Christmas break here, he certainly prepared like he was. As I unpack all the goodies he ordered, and slide the Coke under the tree with a stick-on-bow, my mind wanders, desperately trying to *not* think about what he'd normally be doing over the next few days.

Can I live up to the full spread that his mother produces? Will my last-minute gift hit the spot with that whiskey he likes? Or will this all fall flat on its face…

Looking a the clock, I try to work out what needs doing, and in what order. He'll be late, he always is. So, I lock the door, put the food away, pour myself a glass of chilled Prosecco, and run a bath. Soaking the stress of the last week of school away seems like the perfect start to the Christmas break to me.

It's been one hell of a week, and I wasn't wrong: the kids couldn't care less about the holiday. They're only interested in what they'll get from it and the time they won't have to spend in school. *Sounds about right*. And, whilst I'm an adult and shouldn't care about these things, I can't help but be a little sad about the childhood they're missing.

The popcorn strings they won't be making to decorate their Christmas tree, or the paper chains trailing down the banister. No, their homes will be professionally decorated for the season and picture perfect. Done by someone else.

It's marvellous and sad, all at the same time.

Climbing out of the bath, I dry and slip on my favourite

little black dress before styling my hair and doing my makeup. We might not be together-together, but Christmas Eve drinks at the little cocktail bar down the road is practically a tradition now, no matter what La Famiglia have him doing beforehand.

It might only be for ten minutes, or as much as a couple of hours, but we always make it. Yet, as the time ticks on, I begin to wonder if I've got it wrong. If this is the year I become just another La Famiglia groupie, waiting at home for a man that was never hers in the first place… or maybe that's just the wine talking.

I'm deep in a book when the door slams behind me with, "Ho, ho, ho" coming from the doorway.

Stuffing a receipt in the pages, I drop it on the cushion and peek over the back of the sofa to find Franky in a full Santa costume, complete with Christmas sack.

"So, tell me, little girl… have you been good this year?" he asks.

I'm not sure whether I'm more amused or confused when he drops the bag next to me, then lifts me effortlessly into his lap.

"Girls that don't answer Santa end up on the naughty list, you know?" The tempting promise on his lips has me smiling.

"Where on earth did you get this?" I ask.

"I don't know what you mean, little girl. This is what Father Christmas looks like. Mrs Clause ironed it just this morning. But what happens on the road stays on the road." He winks.

Pushing down a chuckle, I can't help the amused smile

that springs to life.

"Well, then, I've been a very good girl," I reply, snuggling into the soft fabric of his suit. "But my err… my friend… well, he's late, and we're supposed to be going out," I say, playing along.

"Your friend sends his apologies," he replies. "But you've got me tonight instead."

"I'm sure he does." I nod. "He's always so polite." Outside of the bedroom.

"So, you've been a good girl, huh? Do you think you should get a reward for that?"

"You're Father Christmas. You know whether I'm on the nice or naughty list."

"I sure fucking do," he growls, nuzzling the big, fake beard into my neck.

"I'm pretty sure you're not supposed to swear," I whisper.

"With an ass like this in my lap, how could I not?"

"You're incorrigible." I laugh.

"Right," he says, tapping my hip. "Show me this gorgeous outfit—the one your friend is missing out on—and I'll be sure to let him know how stupid he was to pass this evening up."

With a roll of my eyes, I stand, giving him a twirl, my skirt puffing out around me. He nods, appreciation clear on his handsome face, even when it is half hidden under an oversized Christmas hat and a fluffy beard.

"So, some kind of reward," he ponders. "Your friend may have suggested just the thing."

"Did he now?" I ask, picking up my glass of Prosecco.

"And, as this is a one-night only event, a momento might be useful, too. Check the bag."

After taking a sip of my drink, I leave it on the table before warily opening the drawstring bag, then rummaging around with one hand whilst I watch the excited grin on his face. He knows the second I find it, my fingers wrapping around the cylindrical object and pulling it out. *What on earth?*

"Clone a willy…" I read.

"Glow in the dark," he adds with a nod.

"And a vibrating function, too," I say, reading the packet. "You've really covered all the bases here."

"Your friend thought you might like to remember your night with Father Christmas, seeing as he works such strange hours."

"Of course." I nod seriously, pushing down the grin desperate to break free. "Right then. I guess you'd better get it out," I say, looking at his pants.

"Comments like that are not going to get you on the nice list," he says, unfastening his belt as he climbs from the sofa. "If you're not good, I'll have to give you a spanking. You'll need a jug," he adds, striding towards the bedroom without a second glance.

"I could think of much worse things than taking a spanking," I mumble with a shrug, half reading the instructions while I ferret out what I'll need from the kitchen and follow him through to the bedroom.

This is not the strangest thing he's ever brought home. I think that title goes to the sex position dice or the underbed restraints. Both solid choices, in my opinion, but neither of which I'd want to open in front of my parents or friends. I guess we're lucky tonight that it's just Santa and me.

I chuckle to myself. Of course, when I get there, he's laid out on the bed with the lighting dimmed, his jacket open, and his trousers folded neatly on the side.

If I wasn't so distracted by the sight of him lazily stroking his dick, I'd have laughed out loud. The bushy beard hangs half way down his chest, and he has his glorious abs on display.

Shit, it got hot in here.

"If you're going to use this thing, your friend wants it to be the best version possible," he says seriously, getting harder while I stand and watch him.

"It's not quite the *cock*tail hour I was expecting…" I comment idly, dropping everything on the bedside table.

"If you'd rather go for a drink, we can totally do that." He sits up and pulls the jacket together, fastening the button even whilst his hard cock bobs infront of him. "But Father Christmas gets a lot of interest this weekend…"

"Shut up." I can't help the laugh that falls from me.

He leans back with a smile, popping that button back open and taking himself in hand again. Surprisingly, it's not as complicated as you might think, and after a few minutes I have everything set out and ready to go.

"I can't believe we're really going to do this," I say with a bemused chuckle. "My Christmas gift was your dick."

"Well, it could be if you'd stop messing about with that and get your sexy ass over here."

With a smile, I stop stalling and slide between his thighs, finding his beard way too distracting when I tempt a peek upwards. Taking over, I smooth my fingers around the thick of him, stroking up and down.

"Can you reach the stuff?" I ask, not looking up. "You'll need to add the water to the mould mix and put it in the tube at some point."

He reaches over, getting it all in place as I tease and stroke, feeling him get closer and closer, despite doing what I've asked, until he's sliding the filled tube down his chest.

He hisses an intake of breath, muttering something about it being fucking cold as I fondle his balls, keeping him hard while we wait for it to set. He slides it off when I kiss him; his beard ticking against my skin. *This is the weirdest Christmas present ever.*

"Does it take long to set?" he asks, pulling back and placing it on the side.

Jumping up, I mix the luminous liquid and pour it into the mould.

"I want to fuck you with it," he continues, undettered.

"Jesus," I say on an exhale of breath. "I have no idea, but I'll stick with the real thing, if you don't mind."

He places a kiss to my cheek with a dark chuckle before disappearing into the bathroom to clean up, still hard, then struts his fine ass back in just as I'm sliding the vibrating base in to it.

"Can you imagine this thing vibrating in that sweet pussy while I fuck your mouth," he says, coming up behind me and wrapping his arms around my waist, his dick grinding against me. "Oh, or your ass. The options…"

"Not tonight, I'm afraid. That thing better be clean and dry before it goes anywhere near me. Just because it says it's done doesn't mean it's going to be safe."

"Sure it does. Come on, it'll be fun."

"Not tonight, Santa," I say with a shake of my head.

"Fine, fine, but you've got to give me something here, girl. You're fucking killing me." The words tumble from him on a rasp as he grips my tits, pulling me back against him, his scratchy beard grating against my skin.

He shrugs the jacket off and places it with the trousers before perching on the edge of the bed. His hands run beneath my skirt, hot against my skin as he squeezes my ass and drags my underwear down.

"That beard has got to go," I say as his fingers tease against my most sensitive flesh and his other hand reaches up to push off a strap, releasing a breast that barely has time to adjust to the change in temperature before it's wrapped in his hot hand.

"I'm not sure how Mrs Clause is gonna feel about that," he replies huskily.

My core clenches, the ache from this morning nothing more than a promise of what's to come as I rest my head back against him and a moan tumbles from me. He shuffles back on the bed, and I turn to straddle his hips, his face burrying in my chest, tickling as a fit of giggles takes over me.

"I can't take you seriously like this."

He slides the hat and beard off, dumping them over the side of the bed before he does the same with my dress, then drags me down to kiss him. His lips are soft, and his hands thread through my hair as he rubs against me, leaving a fire building beneath my skin I know only he can put out.

I'm hot and wet when he eventually pushes up into me, filling me in a way only he can. We rock and glide, our lips pressed together and our bodies moving to a song neither of us can hear, as instinctive as breathing. He pushes, and I pull, the two of us coming together, collapsing into a tangled, sweaty mess in the sheets.

"I still can't believe you dressed up as Santa and gave me your dick as a gift," I say, a giggle breaking free as I rest my head on his arm and throw my leg over his.

"Well, you were so sad this morning about nobody enjoying Christmas anymore, so I did what needed to be done to make you smile again. It worked, too, right?"

"Absolutely."

He traces patterns over my skin with his fingers, almost lulling me to sleep until I remember I got him something, too. "Fancy a drink?"

"Huh?" he asks sleepily.

"I got you a crap present, too. There's lager in the fridge or something under the tree. Go and have look."

"Ooh," he says, sitting up.

He grins, sliding out from beneath me and disappearing down the corridor before returning with my glass of Prosecco topped up, and his favourite whiskey and Coke.

"Now, don't get me wrong, I love a straight whiskey to end the day with, but there's just something about this chemically tasting goodness that hits the spot differently." He struts around the place naked, hanging free as he slides the hat back on with a smirk, handing me the glass and getting comfortable against the headboard. "I thought you hated all this carbonated, e-number-riddled shit?"

"Yeah, well… it's Christmas." I shrug.

"To our bubbly Christmas," he says, tapping the edge of his glass against my Prosecco.

"To our bubbly Christmas," I agree, something warm wrapping itself around me. "So, food and fucking tomorrow, then?" I ask, thinking about the rest of the stuff that turned up tonight.

Maybe my parents will call at some point, they usually do, but then they're not usually on holiday, so perhaps they won't. Or maybe his family will call and we'll have to explain who he's with and where he is instead of with them, but at the end of the day, it'll be the two of us enjoying ourselves and each other, hopefully.

"Sounds perfect," he replies, kissing the top of my head, reaching out for the remote and turning the TV on to find something to watch.

I still have no idea why he keeps his place when he spends most of his time here. We're together as much as two people can be, just without the label.

"Do you want to come with me on Boxing Day to meet mia famiglia?" he asks quietly.

"I thought your sisters were doing their own thing this year?" I ask, absentmindedly watching the TV.

"They are. It's not that family I'd like to introduce you to."

"Oh." I still.

Franky's been involved in bad things since… well, since way before he ought to have been. Even as teenagers, he and his friends had a reputation—an aura about them. His lack of fucks and overwhelming confidence are some of the things that drew me to him in the first place…

But it's always been a part of his life we've kept separate.

The groupies that flock around the men of La Famiglia are younger, eager, offer something fun and disposable, and he went for that for a while. But at some point, he came here more than there, and the lipstick marks and cheap perfume slowed and then stopped.

I wasn't a helpless romantic waiting around for the boy I'd fallen for to grow into a man. No. I went out, I dated, I enjoyed my life, but there was also something about him that kept drawing me back. We never made promises, agreed to be exclusive or whatever. It just kind of happened, and now he wants me to meet La Famiglia. *Fuck.*

"If you're busy or you don't want to, it's completely fine," he says, sitting up and taking a healthy swig of his drink before placing it on the bedside table—the one with all his stuff in it.

"No, I'm free," I reply, swallowing down the panic and fear. "I'd love to."

FOUR
Franky

Darius waves us through the security barrier and I drive into the compound, down the gravel driveway, and park around the side of the house. Her discomfort is rolling off her in waves even I can pick up on.

"If you'd rather not do this, I can take you home."

I wouldn't want to, but I'd do it. I get that this is intimidating from an outside perspective, but this is just family. Just dinner.

"No, I'm good," she says, looking around nervously. "This is important to you. These people are important to you, so it's good. I'm good. Just nervous, that's all. I've never had to go through security to go to dinner before."

"You get used to it." I shrug, having never really noticed them before. It's just always been part of the process. "I've seen you command a room of a dozen horny teenagers without even breaking a sweat. Dinner with mia famiglia will be a breeze." I kiss the back of her hand before climbing out and coming round the side of the car to open her door.

They'll love her.

"We didn't bring a gift," she hisses quietly.

I guide her around the building that was as much my home as my own growing up.

Her steps falter for a second. "Franky, we can't turn up

without a gift."

"Yes, we can." I open the door and step inside the house. We're not guests—not in the traditional sense. This has been a second home for more than just me for as many years as I can remember.

"It's about time you got here," Tia says, appearing from the den in a blur of movement before Vittoria has even closed the door behind us. "Will you do something with Carlos and Anton, please? I'm trying to coordinate this dinner, and they're hovering about being pests." She stops, her hands full of god knows what as her gaze connects with something or someone over my shoulder. "Oh, Senorita Esposita…"

"It's just Vittoria now we're not in school," she says meekly, sliding her fingers through mine and coming to my side. "You have a beautiful home."

"I do, thank you, but this is my parents' place. Cian and I live nearby," Tia rambles, scrambling to get her thoughts together. I can't help the smile that creeps over my face. Never in my life have I made that woman scramble for words like this. "Uh, is Senorita… I mean *Vittoria* your plus one?"

"Yep." I grin, pulling Vittoria closer into my side. "Is that okay?"

"What on earth is going on here?" Francesca asks as she rushes down the stairs. "That food isn't going to cook itself, Tia, and I've never seen people eat so much food as they do here."

She doesn't even realise Vittoria's someone new as she ushers the two of them into the kitchen, dismissing me completely. I follow them, keen to see what happens when she walks in.

The stunned and confused looks on all the guys' faces are totally worth keeping her a secret once Tia introduces her to her mother and Niamh, with Elena recognising Vittoria eventually with a smile and blush.

A lot of things have changed since we were at school. She was a newbie teacher attempting to wrangle us into something like competent adults, but she looks perfectly at home in the kitchen with Alessia and everyone else.

It's not the kitchen. She'd look just as perfect in an evening gown with a glass of wine, or cuddled up in the den watching a film. She just… fits.

The boys follow me as I make my way to the den, likely looking for answers. Cian and Tino are already in there, mid-conversation, when the questions start flying.

"It's not of your fucking business, and yes, she's here with me," I say, cutting off most of their babbling.

"Who?" Cian asks, looking up.

"One of our old teachers," Carlos says with a smirk.

"The one he used to have a regular Tuesday night study group with," Anton continues.

"No way," Tino says. "You brought Senorita Esposita for dinner with us? That's ballsy beyond measure, my friend." He high fives me, and I flop into one of the bean bags.

"You were fucking a teacher?" Cian confirms. "A teacher?"

"She's not that much older than us, and trust me, it was worth it. She's also not my teacher anymore," I reply with a smile. "But she's also pretty fucking amazing, and I think it's about time you all got to see that. Hell knows, I've had more than enough of all your relationship dramas over the last few years."

"Speaking of relationship drama and the family we never really wanted. are we all ready for the thing later on?" Carlos asks, back to work, once again. Such a busybody.

"Yeah, it's all set up and ready to go," Tino confirms lazily.

"Good," Anton says with a nod. "Once we've got Andrew confirmed in Famiglia Mariotti, that makes everything much simpler."

It's not just that Andrew took over some of our money laundering from his father and he hates it, or that his sister is going to be marrying Carlos – the should-be heir to the Mariotti throne—or that the mother of his child is a solicitor, even if she does specialise in divorce proceedings rather than criminal activities, but the combination means that he's a risk. Not one anyone is willing to leave untethered for much longer.

It should be straight forward. His father was a member. Tying him into us mitigates those apparent risks somewhat. It's join us or don't, but there are consequences to that that I'm reasonably sure a new father isn't going to be willing to take on.

"Sounds good," I agree.

And just like that, we settle in with a drink, leaving the work for later and the girls to it in the kitchen. They wouldn't let us help, even if we offered, and we have, on more than one occasion. There are no more questions about Vittoria and me; no inquisition, just acceptance.

I check in on her more than once, and each time I find her laughing and joking, settling in perfectly, just like I knew she would. I barely make it part way to her before being ushered out of the way and leaving her with nothing more than a smile and a wink.

We're called through to dinner eventually, and, as we pass it, Luca and Andre appear from Luca's office alongside Anton's father, the three of them whispering together quietly. Then, before there's time to question what the three of them are conspiring about, we're seated, eating, and laughing, finally feeling complete with Vittoria at my side and mia famiglia around me.

It doesn't matter that there's work to be done later, even on Boxing Day, or that there are security posted everywhere around the house. We're safe and together, and for the first time, I'm not alone wondering what she's doing or if she's thinking of me like I'm thinking of her.

Finally, we have our very own bubbly family Christmas.

The End

ABOUT THE AUTHOR

H.L. Packer is, quite frankly, a busy bee.

An avid reader as a child, her love for all things written waned into adulthood, the excitement of real life things taking over. But when her life slowed down as she finished her office job for maternity leave, her husband purchased her an e-reader, and that obsession was rekindled.

Quickly she went from reader to reviewer, and then from reviewer to blogger; street teams and promo tours galore. When she began collating her own book boxes over at Romance Readers Book Box UK and had the opportunity to include her own words and worlds, the characters began talking.

Those cheeky characters quickly found themselves written down on the page, and her first series was in progress.

When she is not coordinating her worlds, you can find her running around after her free-spirited three children, and husband, or tending to the dogs, bearded dragons, and snakes that also reside with them.

A break can be found soaking in a bubble bath or enjoying a glass of wine, often still with a book in her hand.

Newsletter: https://bit.ly/3rdYAny

Also by H.L. Packer

Fated Series

Home

Within Reach

Within Hope

The Shadow

Amore

La Familglia

The Ties that Bind

The Bonds That Break

Pendleton Prep

The Sect

Her Devil

His Angel

Their Hell

Printed in Great Britain
by Amazon

51788501R00031